Phonics Focus: long a (ay)

THE RAY

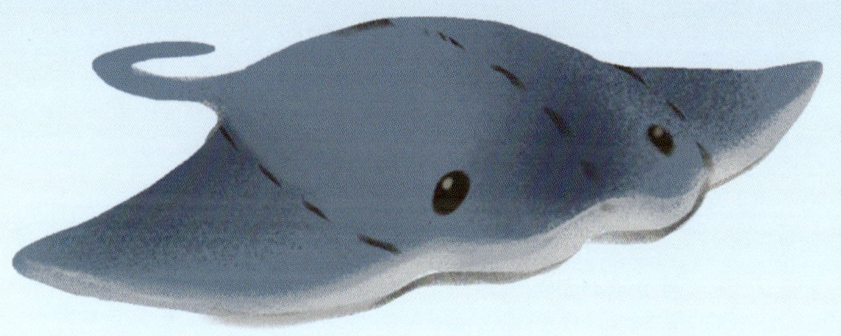

BY CHRISTINA EARLEY

ILLUSTRATED BY
ANASTASIA KLECKNER

A Blue Marlin Book

Introduction:

Phonics is the relationship between letters and sounds. It is the foundation for reading words, or decoding. A phonogram is a letter or group of letters that represents a sound. Students who practice phonics and sight words become fluent word readers. Having word fluency allows students to build their comprehension skills and become skilled and confident readers.

Activities:

BEFORE READING

Use your finger to underline the key phonogram in each word in the *Words to Read* list on page 3. Then, read the word. For longer words, look for ways to break the word into smaller parts (double letters, word I know, ending, etc.).

DURING READING

Use sticky notes to annotate for understanding. Write questions, make connections, summarize each page after it is read, or draw an emoji that describes how you felt about different parts.

AFTER READING

Share and discuss your sticky notes with an adult or peer who also read the story.

Key Word/Phonogram: ray

Words to Read:

bay	tray	playpen
day	archway	playroom
jay	birthday	raceway
May	chambray	saying
ray	delay	stairway
way	dismay	stingrays
yay	hallway	subway
brayed	hooray	today
gray	pathway	Adjatay
prayed	playground	daydreaming

Adjatay woke up and looked at the calendar.

It was May 5th.

"Hooray! Today is my birthday," he thought to himself. "It will be such a good day! But first, I need my lucky toy ray. Where is it?"

AQUARIUM
MAY
S M T W T F S
1 2 3 4 5 6 7
B-DAY
8 9 10 11 12 13 14
15 16 17 18 19 20 21
22 23 24 25 26 27 28
29 30 31

Adjatay looked in the hallway.

Was it on the gray tray? Was it under the archway?

No lucky ray.

Adjatay looked in the playroom.

He looked in the chambray toy box. He looked by the raceway. He looked in his baby sister's playpen.

No lucky ray.

He felt dismay!

Then, Adjatay remembered.

Without delay, he ran down the stairway and out to the playground. On the way, he saw a blue jay on the pathway. It had taken his ray.

"Yay! I have found my lucky ray!" Adjatay shouted.

"Adjatay!" his mother brayed.

Adjatay woke up. He was daydreaming!

"Did you hear what I was saying?" his mother asked. "For your birthday, we will take the subway to see the stingrays in the bay."

"Yay! This is the day I prayed for!" Adjatay cheered.

HAPPY BIRTHDAY
MAY
B-DAY
AQUARIUM
STINGRAY IN THE BAY

Quiz:

1. True or false? Adjatay finds his toy on the playground.
2. True or false? May 5th is Adjatay's birthday.
3. True or false? Adjatay was dreaming.
4. How do you think Adjatay felt when he learned he was going to see stingrays? How do you know?
5. What is one character trait Adjatay has? How do you know?

Flip the book around for answers!

Answers:

1. False
2. True
3. True
4. Possible answer: Happy, because he says, "This is the day I prayed for!"
5. Possible answer: Determined, because he keeps looking for his ray.

Activities:

1. Write a story about Adjatay's day at the bay celebrating his birthday.
2. Write a new story using some or all of the "ay" words from this book.
3. Create a vocabulary word map for a word that was new to you. Write the word in the middle of a paper. Surround it with a definition, illustration, sentence, and other words related to the vocabulary word.
4. Make a song to help others learn the long a sound of "ay."
5. Design a game to practice reading and spelling words with "ay."

Written by: Christina Earley
Illustrated by: Anastasia Kleckner
Design by: Rhea Magaro-Wallace
Editor: Kim Thompson
Educational Consultant: Marie Lemke, M.Ed.
Series Development: James Earley

Library of Congress PCN Data
The Ray (ay) / Christina Earley
Blue Marlin Readers
ISBN 978-1-6389-7998-2 (hard cover)
ISBN 979-8-8873-5057-8 (paperback)
ISBN 979-8-8873-5116-2 (EPUB)
ISBN 979-8-8873-5175-9 (eBook)
Library of Congress Control Number: 2022944996

Printed in China.

Seahorse Publishing Company
seahorsepub.com

Published in the United States
Seahorse Publishing
PO Box 771325
Coral Springs, FL 33077